YASMIN

The Gardener

written by
SAADIA FARUQI

illustrated by
HATEM ALY

PICTURE WINDOW BOOKS
a capstone imprint

To Mariam for inspiring me, and Mubashir
for helping me find the right words—S.F.

To my sister, Eman, and her amazing girls,
Jana and Kenzi—H.A.

Yasmin is published by Picture Window Books, an imprint of Capstone.
1710 Roe Crest Drive
North Mankato, Minnesota 56003
www.capstonepub.com

Text copyright © 2020 by Saadia Faruqi.
Illustrations copyright © 2020 by Capstone.

Library of Congress Cataloging-in-Publication Data is available on
the Library of Congress website.
ISBN: 978-1-5158-4641-3 (hardcover)
ISBN: 978-1-5158-5885-0 (paperback)
ISBN: 978-1-5158-4646-8 (eBook PDF)

Summary: It's spring! Yasmin and her baba are excited to plant their
garden, and Yasmin chooses a flower seedling. She gives it plenty of
sun, water, and good soil . . . so why is it wilting? Watching Nani sit in
the sun gives Yasmin a bright idea, and she knows just what her little
plant needs.

Editorial Credits:
Kristen Mohn, editor; Lori Bye and Kay Fraser, designers; Jo Miller,
media researcher; Tori Abraham, production specialist

Design Elements:
Shutterstock: Art and Fashion, rangsan paidaen

Printed in the United States of America.
PA100

TABLE OF CONTENTS

CHAPTER 1

Spring Is Here

"Spring is my favorite time of the year!" Mama said one day as she looked out the window.

"Why?" asked Yasmin.

Mama pointed to the sky. "The birds are flying about. And everything is green again!"

Baba nodded. "It's the perfect time to plant our garden!"

"Can I help?" Yasmin asked.

"Of course!" Baba said.

Baba and Yasmin went to the garden store. It was full of spring displays. Sunflowers. Roses. Baby trees.

"This is amazing," Yasmin whispered.

Baba bought some vegetable seeds. Carrots, lettuce, tomatoes, and peppers. He also bought soil and a new watering can.

Yasmin saw small pots of flowering plants all in a row.

"Can I please buy a plant, Baba?" Yasmin asked.

"Only if you promise to take care of it," Baba replied. "A plant is a living thing. You must look after it just like a mama would look after a baby."

Yasmin nodded. "I will, I promise."

CHAPTER 2

Planting Seeds

Baba and Yasmin spent the next day in the garden. It was hard work.

Baba dug holes in the soil, and Yasmin dropped seeds into them.

They covered up the holes
with new soil.

Then they watered the area.

"Grow quickly, little seeds,"

Yasmin whispered.

Next Baba helped Yasmin with her flowers. She chose a perfect place near the window. She could look at them whenever she wanted.

"I'm going to water you every day. I'll take care of you, just like a mama and a baba," Yasmin said to her flowers.

The next day Yasmin peeked out the window. Her plants were wilting! The leaves drooped, and the flowers looked sad.

"Oh no," Yasmin cried,
rushing outside. "Maybe the
plants need water!"

She gave her flowers a drink.

The next day she checked

again. They were still wilting.

"Maybe they weren't thirsty,"

she said. "Maybe they need new

soil."

She asked Baba for another scoop of soil. Then she patted the soil around the plants.

On the third day, the plants
were even more wilted. The little
flowers were almost gone.

"What is wrong with my
plants?" cried Yasmin. "I've been
a terrible mama!"

CHAPTER 3

Too Hot

After lunch Nana and Nani came outside to the garden.

"Look at the bright sunshine," Nana said. "I love how it warms my bones."

Nani sat down on a chair and fanned herself.

"The sunshine is making me *too* hot!" she complained.

"Yasmin, can you bring your Nani an umbrella, please?" Baba asked. "It will give her a little shade."

Yasmin went inside to the coat closet. She stared at the umbrellas, wondering. It was too hot and sunny for Nani. Was it also too hot and sunny for the flowers?

Yasmin had an idea.

"Here is a big umbrella for Nani," Yasmin said when she got back to the garden.

"Shukriya, Yasmin," Nani replied.

"And a little umbrella for my flowers," Yasmin said.

She put the small umbrella over her plants.

Nana clapped his hands. "Excellent idea, Yasmin jaan!" he said.

Yasmin smiled. "Let's wait and see."

The next day Yasmin and her parents went outside. Her flowers looked happy and healthy.

"Hooray, I'm a good mama after all!" Yasmin said.

Think About It, Talk About It

* Yasmin's family likes to garden together. If you could grow anything you wanted in a garden, what would you grow and why?

* Yasmin likes to solve her own problems. How would this story be different if Yasmin's baba had found the solution to the plant problem instead of Yasmin? How might Yasmin feel?

* List some ways that Yasmin is helpful in this story. Who or what does she help and how?

Learn Urdu with Yasmin!

Yasmin's family speaks both English and Urdu. Urdu is a language from Pakistan. Maybe you already know some Urdu words!

baba (BAH-bah)—father

hijab (HEE-jahb)—scarf covering the hair

jaan (jahn)—life; a sweet nickname for a loved one

kameez (kuh-MEEZ)—long tunic or shirt

lassi (LAH-see)—yogurt drink

mama (MAH-mah)—mother

nana (NAH-nah)—grandfather on mother's side

nani (NAH-nee)—grandmother on mother's side

salaam (sah-LAHM)—hello

shukriya (shuh-KREE-yuh)—thank you

Pakistani Fun Facts

Yasmin and her family are proud of their Pakistani culture. Yasmin loves to share facts about Pakistan!

Location

Pakistan is on the continent of Asia, with India on one side and Afghanistan on the other.

Islamabad

PAKISTAN

Population

Pakistan's population is more than 200,000,000 people. It is the world's sixth-most-populous country.

Nature

A quarter of Pakistani land is used for agriculture.

Pakistan is home to the second largest juniper forest in the world.

Jasmine is one of the most popular flowers in Pakistan. Yasmin's name means jasmine in Urdu!

Toilet Paper Roll Planters

SUPPLIES:

- 6 empty toilet paper rolls
- ruler
- scissors
- duct tape
- spoon
- potting soil
- seeds of your choice
- small shoebox-size plastic container

STEPS:

1. Using the ruler and scissors, make four 1/4-inch-long cuts around one end of each toilet paper roll.

2. Fold each cut strip inward until they begin to overlap, creating a solid bottom. Use duct tape to strengthen the bottom of each roll.

3. Use the spoon to fill each roll with soil, nearly to the top.

4. Tuck a few seeds into the soil in each roll.

5. Put the rolls in the plastic container and place it near a sunny window inside. Sprinkle with water daily. (Read the instructions on the seed packet for more care instructions.)

6. Watch your garden grow!

Saadia Faruqi is a Pakistani American writer, interfaith activist, and cultural sensitivity trainer previously profiled in *O Magazine*. She is editor-in-chief of *Blue Minaret*, a magazine for Muslim art, poetry, and prose. Saadia is also author of the adult short story collection, *Brick Walls: Tales of Hope & Courage from Pakistan*. Her essays have been published in *Huffington Post*, *Upworthy*, and *NBC Asian America*. She resides in Houston, Texas, with her husband and children.